Superfairies

Sonny the Daring Squirrel

by Janey Louise Jones

illustrated by Jennie Poh

PICTURE WINDOW BOOKS
a capstone imprint

Superfairies is published by Picture Window Books
A Capstone Imprint
1710 Roe Crest Drive
North Mankato, Minnesota 56003
www.mycapstone.com

Library of Congress Cataloging-in-Publication Data

Names: Jones, Janey, 1968- author. | Poh, Jennie, illustrator. |
Jones, Janey, 1968- Superfairies.
Title: Sonny the daring squirrel / by Janey Louise Jones ;
illustrated by Jennie Poh.
Description: North Mankato, Minnesota : Picture Window
Books, a Capstone imprint, [2016] | Series: Superfairies |
Summary: When Sonny the baby squirrel tries to impress his
friends by jumping from the top of a tall oak tree, it almost
ends in disaster, and it is up to the superfairies to comfort the
frightened youngster and restore calm to the forest.
Identifiers: LCCN 2016007953 | ISBN 9781515804338
(library binding : alk. paper) | ISBN 9781515804352 (pbk. :
alk. paper) | ISBN 9781515804376 (ebook pdf : alk. paper)
Subjects: LCSH: Squirrels--Juvenile fiction. | Fairies--Juvenile
fiction. Forest animals--Juvenile fiction. | CYAC: Squirrels--
Fiction. | Fairies--Fiction. | Forest animals--Fiction.
Classification: LCC PZ7.J72019 So 2016 | DDC [E]--dc23 LC
record available at http://lccn.loc.gov/2016007953

Designer: Alison Thiele

For Emilia and Isla
– Janey Louise Jones

For Mum and Dad x
– Jennie Poh

Printed in China.
009694F16

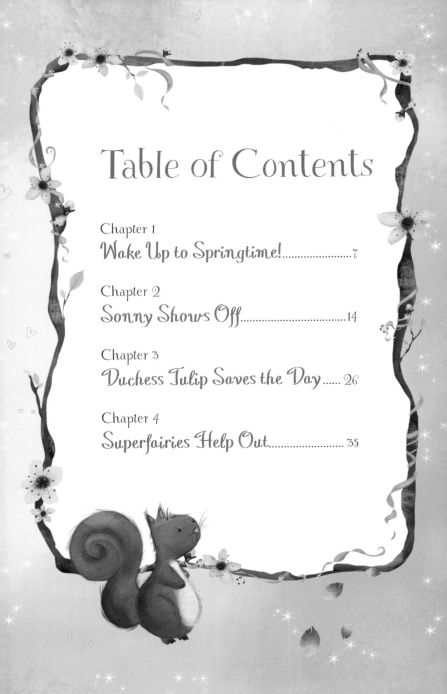

Table of Contents

The Fairy World

The Superfairies of Peaseblossom Woods use teamwork to rescue animals in trouble. They bring together their special superskills, petal power, and lots of love.

Superfairy Rose
can blow super healing fairy kisses to make the animals in Peaseblossom Woods feel better.

Superfairy Berry can see for miles around with her super eyesight.

Superfairy Star can create super dazzling brightness in one dainty spin to lighten up dark places.

Superfairy Silk spins super strong webs for animal rescues.

Chapter 1

Wake Up to Springtime!

Pink blossoms bloomed on the cherry blossom tree, which meant it was time for Duchess Tulip to visit the Superfairies in Peaseblossom Woods.

The four Superfairies were getting ready for her visit and a busy time ahead. The animals of Peaseblossom Woods were waking up after a long winter sleep. There would be more rescues for sure!

The four Superfairies—Rose, Berry, Star, and Silk—were looking at their springtime dresses in their wardrobes.

"We don't need our cosy winter clothes anymore!" said Star with a twirl. "I can't wait to wear my petal dresses without a cape! Spring clothes are so pretty!"

Silk spotted a curious-looking box next to the spring shoes.

"I wonder what's in that?" she said, fluttering toward it and taking off the lid.

"Oh! Look at this scrapbook I made about Duchess Tulip's last visit," she said, taking a petal-covered book from the box.

Rose, Berry, and Star gathered around to see the pictures sketched by Silk. There were scraps of twigs, leaves, and blossom petals saved from the last visit.

"Ooh, I love it when Duchess Tulip comes!" said Star. "She always brings sunshine and gentle breezes with her. And a few showers, of course!"

"We must make elderflower tea and rosehip honeybuns!" said Berry. "She loves those!"

"Yes," said Rose, "and we'll do the maypole dance with her as usual. That's always so fun. Oh, that reminds me—we should decorate the maypole."

"Where are the ribbons?" asked Silk.

"In our spring cabinet," said Rose, fluttering over to find them.

"Tada!" said Rose, finding the ribbons in spring colors—yellow, pink, blue, and green.

The four Superfairies flew outside and attached colorful ribbons to the maypole.

In the heart of the woods, on
Lavender Lane, the little animals were
delighted to be wide awake after the
long, quiet winter rest. The young friends
danced through the woods, singing silly
songs as they went.

Sonny Squirrel was the youngest of all the animals, and he was all alone.

His mother had sent him out to collect twigs because he'd been pestering her to get outside.

"Don't go where you can't see our house!" his mother had warned.

But Sonny wandered farther through the woods, noticing the others having fun.

"Hey, can I join in?" he called.

"No, your legs are too short to keep up with us!" Basil Bear said with a laugh.

"Yeah, you're just a baby," said Billy Badger.

Sonny's sister, Susie, looked a little worried about him, but she didn't want to make a fuss in case the others laughed.

"I am not a baby!" said Sonny angrily.

"Prove it, then!" said Basil Bear.

Chapter 2

Sonny Shows Off

"Well," said Sonny, thinking hard.

"Yes?" said Basil with a smirk on his face.

"You see that log over there?" said Sonny.

"What about it?" said Billy Badger.

"I could jump off that!" said Sonny.

"Try it, then!" said Billy.

Sonny ran over to the log and flung himself onto it.

The other animals giggled because he looked so funny, trying to scramble onto the top of the log.

Once he was standing on it, he
counted to three and . . .

Jump!

He landed on the woodland floor.

"Told you I could!" said Sonny with a
wide grin.

"Anyone could do that!" said Basil.

"Leave him alone," said Martha Mouse. "He's just a baby."

"I AM NOT A BABY!" cried Sonny.

He was going to have to work harder to get the respect of the big boys.

Sonny looked around for ideas.

"You see the first branch of the tree up there?" he said, looking up at the lowest branch of a big oak tree. "I could jump from that!"

"I'd like to see you try!" said Basil.

Little Sonny darted up the tree trunk to the first branch. He crawled along it on his tummy. *Oh no, it's a long way down from here*, he thought. *Why did I say I'd jump?*

Poor little Sonny gathered all his courage and one, two, three . . .

Jump!

He was scared as he fell, but he didn't show it.

Phew, I made it, he thought as he landed on the ground with a thud.

"Anyone could jump from the first branch," said Basil with a snicker.

"Yeah, we did that when we were much younger than you!" said Billy.

Sonny was so disappointed that the older boys did not admire him like he had hoped. Instead of giving in, he tried to think of a more impressive stunt that he could do.

"I can climb to the very top of the tree and jump off! I won't even get scared! I've done it lots of times," boasted Sonny, who was telling lies now.

"Go ahead, then," said Basil. "I'd like to see this."

"No, Sonny!" cried Susie. "You will get hurt, and Mom and Dad will be angry with you. Plus, I will get in tons of trouble for not stopping you!"

"Well, don't watch," said Sonny. "Then you can't be blamed for not stopping me!"

Susie and Martha went down to the riverbank. They couldn't bear to watch Sonny trying to impress Basil and Billy.

"The thing is," said Martha. "Even if they were impressed, they'd never admit it, so Sonny is wasting his time."

"Exactly," agreed Susie. "I'm very annoyed with Basil and Billy!"

Back at Lavender Lane, Sonny bravely started to make his way up the trunk of the huge tree. His little heart thumped in his chest as he clambered to the top.

He slipped . . . but he held on. Up and up and up he went.

As he got higher and higher, Sonny felt dizzier and dizzier.

Oh no! he thought. *Why did I say that I've done this lots of times? I've never even done it once before. I'm very scared.*

Once he was on a very high branch, the woodland floor looked like such a long way down. It was too far to jump.

What will I do? he thought.

"Go, Sonny!" cried Billy.

Susie and Martha could hear what was going on. They made their way back to see Sonny.

Sonny began to feel dizzy with fear as he swung back and forth. He clung onto the branch.

Everyone could see that it was too high.

"Don't do it!" cried Susie.

"Come down, Sonny!" called Basil from below. "You will hurt yourself if you jump."

But Sonny didn't want to fail. He closed his eyes and tiptoed along to the tip of the branch.

If I scramble down now, they will think I'm a coward. They will never let me play with them, Sonny thought.

So he stepped off the branch into midair.

"*Aaarggghh!*" cried Sonny as he hurtled toward the ground, doing somersaults as he went.

"No!" sobbed Susie.

"Oh, Sonny!" cried Basil and Billy, feeling very worried and guilty.

The four friends felt helpless as they watched Sonny fall.

Chapter 3

Duchess Tulip Saves the Day

Duchess Tulip flew through the woods carrying gifts for the Superfairies. She flew so fast that if you blinked, you'd miss her. But she brought with her the air of spring, and the woods started to sparkle with clear, yellow sunlight.

She approached Lavender Lane just as Sonny was mid-tumble.

"Tra-la-la-la ..." she sang to herself.

Suddenly, up ahead, she saw little
Sonny tumbling down from the treetop,
as if in slow motion.

"Oh no!" she cried.

All the little animals looked on in
horror as Sonny fell. They scrambled
around, trying to figure out the best spot
to catch him.

But before Sonny reached the ground, he hit a springy branch and bounced off it . . .

Bounce!

Then sprang back upward into the tree . . .

Boing!

Ending up right inside the nest of a mother bird and her five babies with a

bump-thud!

The baby birds all went squawk!

They made a lot of noise because they had no idea what had hit them. It's not every day that a squirrel ends up in the middle of a bird's nest!

Duchess Tulip couldn't quite believe her eyes.

The babies flapped into a panic! A mass of fluffy feathers exploded as the five little birds tried to fly away from

Sonny, even though their wings were not
strong enough.

Duchess Tulip didn't know who to help first! She laid down her gifts, getting ready for action.

"I'm going to need as much help as possible with this problem!" she said as the birds half-flew and half-ran away from their nest, along branches of the big tree.

Duchess Tulip rang the bells for the Superfairies. Then she flew up to the nest, speaking gently to Sonny and the birds.

"Hey, let's get this little squirrel out of there so you can have some peace, okay?" she said.

Sonny nodded gratefully, as did the mother bird, who was desperately trying to round her chicks back together.

Duchess Tulip carried poor, confused Sonny down to the woodland floor. He was very unsteady on his feet—his head was still spinning from the fall.

"Lie down by this tree," said Duchess Tulip, "and take nice calm breaths."

Susie and Martha came racing over to look after him.

"Oh, Sonny!" said Susie, hugging her brother. "I'm so glad you are okay. I feel terrible for letting this happen!"

"I'm okay," said Sonny, clinging to his big sister. "But I'd like to see Mommy and Daddy!"

Basil and Billy looked very sorry indeed.

"I feel so bad!" said Basil.

"Me too!" said Billy. "We should never have let him go way up the tree. He was trying to impress us!"

Basil nodded. "We should have said 'Good job!' for jumping off the log. That was enough for a little squirrel to do!"

"You are right, boys," said Duchess Tulip. "Luckily, he's okay. You should have taken care of Sonny. Do you promise nothing like this will happen again?"

Basil and Billy nodded.

"I think you mean it. Now, run off and play nicely in the sunshine. I still have work to do here."

Duchess Tulip went to help round up the baby birds.

"Come on, little ones," Duchess Tulip said softly. "I will take you back to your nest."

But they were scared and hid stubbornly in tiny holes dotted all over the tree.

"Oh dear!" said their mother. "They won't come out!"

Chapter 4

Superfairies Help Out

There was a cheer from the animals as the Superfairies' fairycopter landed.

Rose, Berry, Silk, and Star flew to the oak tree.

"Hello, Duchess Tulip!" they cried.

"Hello, Superfairies!" replied Duchess Tulip. "Things have gone wrong here. Poor Sonny needs some loving care, and the baby birds are too nervous to come out of hiding."

Rose went straight to see Sonny, blowing him healing kisses.

"Oh, I'm feeling better already!" he said.

Soon he felt well enough for Susie to take him home.

"Now let's think about what we should do for the birds," said Duchess Tulip.

"I could search for the birds with my super eyesight," offered Berry.

"A good plan—that will be part of what we need to do. But it doesn't help get them out of their hiding holes," said Duchess Tulip.

"I could make some Rescue Silk for them to climb along," suggested Silk.

"True. And that's a great idea. But they are so tiny, they could fall through the gaps," said Duchess Tulip.

"Maybe I could dazzle them," volunteered Star.

"A nice idea. But it might startle them rather than tempt them out," said Duchess Tulip.

"What about my healing kisses?" said Rose.

"Lovely, but only once we've gotten them safely back in the nest," advised Duchess Tulip.

Rose nodded. "I agree. There has to be something that would tempt them out of hiding. That's what we need to think about."

"Oh, please help me get them back,"
said the mother bird. She was getting
very impatient to have all her family back
together. "They will be hungry. I was just
about to go out looking for food when
Sonny landed in the middle of us!"

"Don't worry—we'll rescue them,"
said Rose. "We always do. We have
to think of what's best—not what's
quickest!"

Duchess Tulip flew around in a circle while she thought about what to do.

"I have an idea!" she said. "Superfairies, let's have a team chat. Come and join me!"

The Superfairies gathered around the duchess to hear the plan.

"Let's each take a piece of this tasty bread and see if it can tempt them out of hiding. Their mother said that they are hungry. Food could be just the thing!"

"Great idea, Duchess Tulip!" said Rose.

The Superfairies and Duchess Tulip circled the tree, whispering to the baby birds and offering the scrumptious smelling bread.

"Don't be afraid!" said Duchess Tulip.

At first, there was no response.

Then one little bird poked its head out of its hiding place.

"Peekaboo!" said Rose.

"Oh, hello!" said Star.

And the other little birds soon appeared too!

"Hey, little bird!" said Silk.

"I bet you're hungry!" said Berry.

At last, all the birds were back with their mother.

"Oh, thank you!" cried the mother bird as her babies followed her into the nest. They feasted on even more of the delicious bread.

Rose blew healing kisses to the birds.

"Well, I think it's time we had a snack and caught up on other news!" said Duchess Tulip, feeling satisfied that everyone was okay now.

"That sounds like a lovely idea!" said Rose.

"Why don't you come in the fairycopter over to the cherry blossom tree?" said Superfairy Star. "We can have some rosehip honeybuns and elderflower tea."

"That sounds just great," said Duchess Tulip, flying to the fairycopter with the four Superfairies.

It was time for some springtime fairy fun back at the cherry blossom tree.

After a delicious snack, and lots of chatting, the Superfairies and Duchess Tulip danced around the maypole. And as they did, the animals of Peaseblossom Woods came to join them.

It was time to celebrate the new life of springtime and everyone wanted to dance with Duchess Tulip to welcome in the season. Basil Bear and Billy Badger took especially good care of Sonny Squirrel at the party.

They danced and sang until dark, then fell asleep under the spring stars.

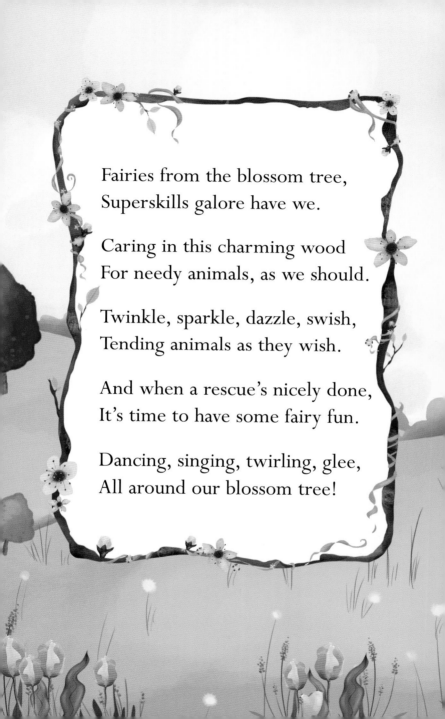

Fairies from the blossom tree,
Superskills galore have we.

Caring in this charming wood
For needy animals, as we should.

Twinkle, sparkle, dazzle, swish,
Tending animals as they wish.

And when a rescue's nicely done,
It's time to have some fairy fun.

Dancing, singing, twirling, glee,
All around our blossom tree!

Glossary

curious (KYUR-ee-uhss)—eager to know or learn something

disappointed (dis-uh-POIN-tid)—sad that something didn't go as you hoped

impressive (im-PRES-iv)—grand or awesome

maypole (MAY-pohl)—a wooden pole for dancing around

respect (ri-SPEKT)—admire someone or something, or be polite

somersault (SUHM-ur-sawlt)—a forward roll

stubborn (STUHB-urn)—refusing to change your mind even when advised to do so

tempt (TEMPT)—encourage someone to do something that might be a bad idea

Talk It Out

1. Do you wear different clothes when the weather is warmer, just like the Superfairies do? What do you wear in springtime?

2. Why do you think people show off, boast, and pretend they can do things they can't really do? Have you ever been a show-off? How could it be dangerous to lie that you can do certain things?

Write It Down

1. Sonny tells lies in order to sound "cool." Write about a time when you told a lie. Explain why you lied, how it made you feel, and if you have ever lied since.

2. With a friend, make a magazine all about spring. It might have a quiz about spring, a crossword or wordsearch, a story or poem about spring, some pictures, and spring facts! Think of a great name for your magazine, too!

All About Fairies

The legend of fairies is as old as time. Fairy tales tell stories of fairy magic. According to legend, fairies are so small and delicate, and fly so fast, that they might actually be all around us, but just very hard to see. Fairies, supposedly, only reveal themselves to believers.

Fairies often dance in circles at sunrise and sunset. They love to play in woodlands among wildflowers. If you sing gently to them, they may appear.

Here are some of the world's most famous fairies:

The Flower Fairies

Artist Cicely Mary Barker painted a range of pretty flower fairies and published eight volumes of flower fairy art from 1923. The link between fairies and flowers is very strong.

The Tooth Fairy

She visits us during the night to leave money when we lose our baby teeth. Although it is very hard to catch sight of her, children are always happy when she visits.

Fake Fairies

In 1917, cousins Elsie Wright and Frances Griffiths said they photographed fairies in their garden. They later admitted that most were fakes—but Frances claimed that one was genuine.

Which Animal Friend Are You?

1. What is your favorite time of day?
    A) early morning
    B) afternoon
    C) lunchtime!
    D) nighttime

2. When out in the countryside, would you rather:
    A) climb a tree
    B) have a picnic
    C) throw stones in a river
    D) skip through wildflowers

3. Which type of story is best?
    A) adventure
    B) funny
    C) scary
    D) happy

4. Which word describes you?
    A) brave
    B) kind
    C) naughty
    D) gentle

5. If you made a cake for your friends, would it be:
    A) chocolate cake
    B) toffee cake
    C) banana cake
    D) carrot cake

6. If you are having your picture taken, do you:
   A) do something dangerous
   B) smile nicely
   C) make a silly face
   D) put your arm around your friend

7. What's the most fun way to travel?
   A) rocket
   B) train
   C) race car
   D) horse and cart

8. Which of these smells do you prefer?
   A) engine oil
   B) fresh flowers
   C) cut grass in summer
   D) cakes in the oven

Mostly A—you are like Sonny Squirrel. Fun-loving and adventurous, you want to make lots of friends!

Mostly B—you are like Susie Squirrel. You are thoughtful, kind, and loving, but you like to play as well!

Mostly C—you are like Basil Bear. You enjoy exploring new things. You love company and lots of laughs.

Mostly D—you are like Martha Mouse. You are sweet-natured and have lots of feelings for others. You love your friends and spending time with them is your favorite thing!

About the Author

Janey Louise Jones has been a published author for 10 years. Her Princess Poppy series is an international bestselling brand, with books translated into 10 languages, including Hebrew and Mandarin. Janey is a graduate of Edinburgh University and lives in Edinburgh, Scotland with her three sons. She loves fairies, princesses, beaches, and woodlands.

About the Illustrator

Jennie Poh was born in England and grew up in Malaysia (in the jungle). At the age of 10 she moved back to England and trained as a ballet dancer. She studied fine art at Surrey Institute of Art & Design as well as fashion illustration at Central Saint Martins. Jennie loves the countryside, animals, tea, and reading. She lives in Woking, England with her husband and two wonderful daughters.

JOIN THE
Superfairies
ON MORE
MAGICAL
ANIMAL RESCUES!

Basil the Bear Cub
by Jenny Louise Jones

Dancer the Wild Pony
by Jenny Louise Jones

Martha the Little Mouse
by Jenny Louise Jones

Violet the Velvet Rabbit
by Jenny Louise Jones

Sonny the Daring Squirrel
by Jenny Louise Jones

Farrah the Shy Fawn
by Jenny Louise Jones

THE *Fun* DOESN'T STOP HERE!

For MORE GREAT BOOKS go to
WWW.MYCAPSTONE.COM